D1499763

Also by Ingri and Edgar Parin d'Aulaire
Published by the University of Minnesota Press

Children of the Northlights

OLA

by INGRI & EDGAR PARIN D'AULAIRE

University of Minnesota Press
Minneapolis · London

Publisher's Note

At the time this book was written in 1932, the term *Lapp* was commonly used to refer to the Sami people living in the northern regions of Norway, Sweden, Finland, and the Kola Peninsula of Russia. In recent decades the Sami have distanced themselves from this word, considering it a derogatory label rather than a legitimate ethnic description. Our knowledge and appreciation of indigenous peoples have advanced significantly since this book was first published. To remain faithful to the authors' language, *Ola* is reprinted here in its original form as a contribution to Scandinavia's heritage, but we recognize the contemporary preference for *Sami* rather than *Lapp* as the name for this culture.

The University of Minnesota Press gratefully acknowledges assistance provided for the publication of this book by the John K. and Elsie Lampert Fesler Fund.

Originally published in 1932 by Doubleday, Doran & Company, Inc.
First University of Minnesota Press edition, 2013

Copyright 1932 by Ingri and Edgar Parin d'Aulaire
Copyright renewed 1959 by Ingri and Edgar Parin d'Aulaire

All rights reserved. No part of this publication may be reproduced, stored in a retrieval system, or transmitted, in any form or by any means, electronic, mechanical, photocopying, recording, or otherwise, without the prior written permission of the publisher.

Published by the University of Minnesota Press
111 Third Avenue South, Suite 290
Minneapolis, MN 55401-2520
http://www.upress.umn.edu

Library of Congress Cataloging-in-Publication Data
D'Aulaire, Ingri, 1904–1980. D'Aulaire, Edgar Parin, 1898–1986.
Ola / Ingri and Edgar Parin d'Aulaire.—First University of Minnesota Press edition.
Summary: When Ola, a Norwegian boy, dons his skis in search of adventure, he meets new friends, joins a wedding party, encounters a dragon, and learns folklore from fishermen.
ISBN 978-0-8166-9017-6 (hardback)
[1. Adventure and adventurers—Fiction. 2. Norway—History—Fiction.] I. D'Aulaire, Edgar Parin, 1898–1986, joint author. II. Title.
PZ7.A914Ol 2013
[E]—dc232013017254

Printed in China on acid-free paper
The University of Minnesota is an equal-opportunity educator and employer.

20 19 18 17 16 15 14 13   10 9 8 7 6 5 4 3 2 1

Juvenile
PZ
7
.D2646
O42
2013

To Vesle Per . . . . . Mellem Per . . . . . **Gamle Per**

FAR UP IN THE NORTH

the sun is afraid to show his pale face in winter. But the moon and the stars love the sparkling frost. They gleam fairylike through the long night and the arctic lights leap across the sky in cold, silent flames. They glitter on the snow and the ice of a long, mountainous country down below. In their magic light the country looks like a huge silver spoon, thousands of miles long. This is Norway. And it is the strangest country in the world. It is so crowded with mountains, forests, huge trolls, red-capped gnomes, and alluring Hulder-maidens that only a few human people have room to live there.

In this country there is a forest, in winter a very strange forest. For under the

heavy burden of snow the trees turn into a crowd of solemn creatures.

In the middle of the forest there was a small house.

And in this house there lived a small boy. Ola was his name. His eyes were light blue, his tousled hair was yellow, and his face was rosy from much fresh air. With sleepy eyes Ola peered out through the tangle of frost roses on his window.

The flaring arctic lights had awakened him, and he decided to put on his clothes and go out for a while to look around.

Strange adventures might wait for him, behind the quaint paintings on the old door. So he opened the door and went out.

At the gate a moose was standing, and some hares played quietly around Ola while he fastened his skis to his feet.

But when he wanted to join their play they scampered, frightened, to all sides. A small hare was so stupid that it ran just in front of Ola's skis. "Run on, my seven-league boots," said Ola to his skis.

"Let us see if we can catch that hare."

For a long time he followed the hare and could not overtake it. But when he came to a very steep slope, his skis started to race down so fast that they caught up with the hare. Quick-witted Ola squatted down and grabbed it. Down the slope they flew, faster and faster,

and right over a high bank.

Some girls happened to be standing under the bank. When a white hare and a red cap fell at their feet, right from the sky, they were sure it was a gnome who wanted to play hide-and-seek with them.

They looked all over for the gnome. But instead of a gnome they saw Ola high up in a pine tree, hanging by his skis. "I caught hold of these branches," he boasted. "Help me down, you silly girls." So they did. And they told him they were Siri and Turi, Randi and Guri, Mari and Kari and Gro, and he might come along to see a wedding in the next valley.

Ola joined the girls and they rushed down to a big farm where the buildings
played merry-go-round around a birch tree.

From the big storehouse and scullery, maids were carrying all kinds of delicious food. There was butter and brown goat-cheese shaped like animals and castles. There were stacks of flat-bread, large as millstones and thin as leaves, and trout and meat and porridge and cakes. There was also a big bowl of ale, and on its surface swam small drinking vessels like ducks on a pond.

The children heard music from the main house, so they ran to a window and peeped in.

At the fireplace sat an old fiddler, playing and singing, and at a long table the wedding party was seated. The bride looked just like a princess with a huge silver crown on her head, and the groom

had silver buttons wherever there was a place on his suit. The bridal feast was to last for several days, and this was just a light meal to give the wedding party strength for the long ride to church.

When lunch was over the whole party came out and climbed into sleighs.

They started off and the children hung on behind. The girls were soon thrown off; only Ola managed skillfully to keep on. Up hill and down hill they flew.

But suddenly, as they approached the church, a howling black dragon rushed out from a cave. It plowed through the drifts that blocked its way, throwing the

snow this way and that and covering the whole wedding party. "The dragon swallowed me," thought Ola, and he did not dare to move. The parson and the sexton helped the others out of the snow

and they stepped into the church as if nothing had happened. Only a red cap
was left over as it did not belong to any of the party.

After a while Per peddler passed and stopped to pick up the red cap. He was surprised to find a yellow tuft beneath. As he pulled, Ola came up. Ola was afraid Per peddler would laugh at him if he told him about the dragon. So he said: "I just dug myself a house like the Lapps."

"So?" said Per peddler. "But the Lapps don't live like that. They live in tents and have reindeers. I am on my way there now." "Please, peddler, take me along," Ola begged. "All right," said Per peddler. "You may help me carry." They traveled over

mountains and valleys and rivers and lakes, always to the north. The days grew shorter and shorter till at last the sun did not show himself at all. At noon there was just a dim light. The roads ended, but Ola and Per peddler went on and on.

At last they met a Lapp who was herding a flock of reindeer. The deer were all digging for moss under the snow. Nearby were the Lapp tents.

While Per peddler was busy trading, Ola stared at the reindeer and Lapp children just as curiously as they stared at him.

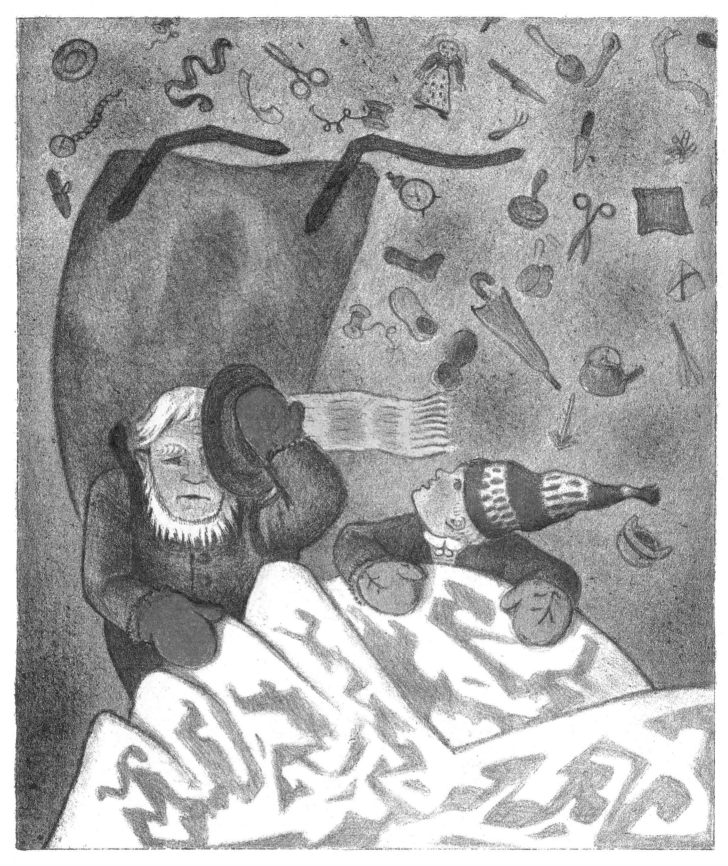

Then Ola and Per peddler went on south again over wild mountains where a furious storm was raging. Suddenly Per peddler's huge knapsack blew open and all his nice goods were scattered about.

Not far away there was a fishing village on the shore of the Arctic Ocean. "Don't worry," said Per to Ola. "While I go to get new goods, you can go fishing."

The first thing Per peddler did when he came to the fishing village was to buy Ola a fisherman's outfit and, dressed in that, Ola at once got work.

All day long he spent out on the fishing grounds, pulling in cod. Ola liked it. Sometimes his boat was deep in a wave valley and the fishermen in the boats nearby looked as if they were sitting in water up to their necks. Sometimes his boat was high on a water mountain and Ola could see hundreds of other fisherboats gathered from all parts of Norway.

The fishermen told Ola that strange people live in small houses at the bottom of the sea, and they have lots of goats grazing on their grass roofs. But these goats are very greedy for the tidbits of the fishing hooks, and to their owners' horror the goats get drawn right up and change into codfish. The fishermen showed Ola bits of goats' beards on the chins of the codfish.

They took Ola to a place where the water was boiling and whirling around a black cliff. "That is the Maelstrom," they said. "Here at the bottom a man and his wife sit quarreling over their huge kettle of food. He stirs this way and she stirs that way, and the water becomes so terribly rough that no ship can sail across."

In the evening when they came back to the harbor, they all worked together, preparing the codfish. They cleaned the fish and hung them on racks to dry, and the livers they steamed into delicious codliver oil. They gave Ola a very large fish for himself and a can of codliver oil.

All of a sudden spring was there. The codfish went off to the great ocean, and the fishermen sold their catch and sailed for their far-away homes.

Ola decided that he would go home, too.

He had heard that he could go most of the way by ship. So as he saw a boat lying deserted at the shore, he crawled into it and rowed off.

He had not rowed far, however, when the wind blew the clouds right down over him. In the fog Ola could not see his hand before his face.

But he rowed on. Suddenly his hair stood upright on his head, for he heard a terrible howl as from many wild animals.

But the fog lifted, and there he saw a boat loaded with cats. "These terrible cats," said the man who rowed the boat, "they are furious because I took them away from the birds' islets so the birds may hatch in peace."

On one of the islets Ola saw a little girl crying. "I want my kitten back," she sobbed. "Never mind," said Ola. "You'll get your kitten back in the fall. Show me the birds now." "All right," said the little girl. "You can help me gather eiderdown. I'll give you an empty sack."

Among the grass and heather the eider ducks were sitting on their nests. The nests were softly lined with down, and the birds did not mind when the children took some of it away.

After they had filled the sacks with down they climbed a steep cliff. Here millions of cormorants, gulls, sea-parrots, and auks had their nests.

At the top of the cliff a crowd of children came running toward them. "Look at our beautiful midnight sun!" they cried. "It won't set for many weeks, and all that time we may be up all night."

Ola looked and saw hundreds of cliffs shaped like strange animals. The red sun rolled along their backs. Suddenly he saw a ship sailing southward between the cliffs, and on deck he recognized Per peddler.

Per peddler had chartered the ship and loaded it with dried cod. Now he was on his way to Bergen to sell it. "Wait, wait," cried Ola, "take me along home!" Per peddler stopped the ship, and the children let Ola down on a rope. The little girl said he might keep the sack with down that he carried.

And
with his down,
his fish, and his codliver oil
Ola boarded the ship
and sailed homeward.

Known for their vibrant and imaginative interpretations of Scandinavian folklore, Greek and Norse mythology, and American history, the books of **Ingri** (1904–1980) and **Edgar Parin d'Aulaire** (1898–1986) have entertained readers for more than seventy-five years. Throughout their career the couple made frequent trips to Norway, where they gathered inspiration for many of their most celebrated books, including *East of the Sun and West of the Moon, Leif the Lucky, d'Aulaires' Book of Norse Myths,* and the perennial favorite, *d'Aulaires' Book of Trolls.* Their colorful portrayal of the Sami people of northern Scandinavia, *Children of the Northlights,* is also available from the University of Minnesota Press. The d'Aulaires received the Caldecott Medal in 1940 for their book *Abraham Lincoln* and were later awarded the Regina Medal for their distinguished contribution to children's literature.